Ted's Week
A lesson on bullying

by Suzanne I. Barchers

illustrated by Mattia Cerato

RED
CHAIR
•PRESS•

Please visit our website at **www.redchairpress.com**.
Find a free catalog of all our high-quality products for young readers.

Ted's Week
Library of Congress Control Number: 2012931801
ISBN: 978-1-937529-17-8 (pbk)
ISBN: 978-1-937529-25-3 (hc)

Lexile is a registered trademark of MetaMetrics, Inc. Used with permission.
Leveling provided by Linda Cornwell of Literacy Connections Consulting.

This edition first published in 2012 by
Red Chair Press, LLC   PO Box 333   South Egremont, MA 01258-0333

Printed in China
1 2 3 4 5 16 15 14 13 12

Bun

Pip

Sox

Tab

Ted

Ted's Week

Monday through Friday, poor Ted is bothered by the blue jays. They swoop, they peck, they tease until Ted's friends help him out one Saturday. Let's find out if Ted can finally take a Sunday stroll without being bothered by the bullies.

Early one Monday, Ted goes for a walk.
Two blue jays see him. They start to talk.

"Let's scare that hedgehog. Let's make him run.
He's too shy to fight us. This could be fun."

The jays fly at Ted. They pick and they push.
Ted rolls in a ball, right into a bush!

Ted stays in that bush. He stays curled up tight.
He misses his dinner. He's had such a fright.

On Tuesday, Ted goes to see his friend Bun.
Those jays see him walking. They want some more fun.

The jays fly at Ted. They cackle with glee.
Ted rolls in a ball, right into a tree!

On Wednesday, Ted wants to see his friend Pip.
He hopes that on this day he'll finish the trip.

But those jays are waiting. They don't give a break.
This time poor Ted rolls right into the lake.

On Thursday Ted goes to see his friend Tab.
But those blue jays tease Ted. They peck and they jab.

Ted hisses and clicks. He feels really bad.
He puffs up his spines. He tries to look mad.

Those blue jays don't care. They think Ted is funny.
"Run along home, kid. You can't scare us, sonny."

Ted sadly heads back home to his place.
One lonely tear rolls right down his face.

On Friday, Ted knows that he must try again.
He hopes he can get as far as Sox's den.

16

He sneaks from his house. He takes a new route.
But those jays are sneakier. They find him out.

Ted puffs up his spines. He hisses and then...
He curls up and rolls—right into Sox's den!

"Teddy," says Sox, "Are you alright?
Did someone chase you? Did you get in a fight?"

"I would never fight," Ted says with a frown.
"But the jays won't stop teasing. It's getting me down."

20

Sox says, "Ted, don't worry. Leave it to me.
Come meet me tomorrow by the big oak tree."

On Saturday, those jays swoop and they dive.
But this time Ted rolls right into a hive!

The bees chase the jays. Each angry bee stings.
The jays screech and cry, flapping their wings.

On Sunday, Ted goes out again for a walk.
He meets all his friends. They walk and they talk.

24

And those two bullies have learned from the bees.
It's not good to play tricks, to be mean, or to tease.

Big Questions:

How does Ted feel when the blue jays bother him? How do you know?

When Ted goes out for his walk next week, do you think the jays will bully him again?

Big Words:

cackle: a loud, mean laugh

fright: a sudden feeling of fear

route: a way down a road or path

The blue jays teased and bothered Ted. Have you ever been teased? How did it make you feel? Do you think it was right that Ted told his friend Sox about how the jays bullied him?

Sox and Ted team up as buddies. Do you think it's a good idea to have a friend or adult buddy when you want to deal with bullies?

A pledge is a promise you make and share with others. On the top of a blank sheet of paper write MY BUDDY PLEDGE. Then write this sentence and complete it: I promise to talk to my buddy _____ if someone is a bully to me. Fill in the blank with the name of a friend, sibling or adult you are close to. Decorate the pledge with crayons and stickers. Share the pledge with your buddy.

About the Author

Suzanne I. Barchers, Ed.D., began a career in writing and publishing after fifteen years as a teacher. She has written over 100 children's books, two college textbooks, and more than 20 reader's theater and teacher resource books. She previously held editorial roles at Weekly Reader and LeapFrog and is on the PBS Kids Media Advisory Board for the next generation of children's programming. Suzanne also plays the flute professionally—and for fun—from her home in Stanford, CA.

About the Illustrator

Mattia Cerato was born in Cuneo, a small town in northern Italy where he still lives and works. As soon as he could hold a pencil he loved sketching things he saw around him. When he is not drawing, Mattia loves traveling around the world, reading good books, and playing and listening to cool music.

 For a free activity page for this story, go to www.redchairpress.com and look for Free Activities.